Damage
Noted
watndamage 8/05 ws

OCT 16 1993

CHILDREN'S DEPARTMENT
NEW BRITAIN PUBLIC LIBRARY
20 HIGH STREET
NEW BRITAIN, CT. 06051

W9-AWW-994

Damage
Noted
watndamage 8/05 ws

The Boy
and the Giants

FIONA MOODIE

Farrar · Straus · Giroux   New York

For Claire

There was once a fisherboy who lived on an island at the edge of the world. His name was Thomas and he loved a girl named Kate. They would have been very happy, except for the terrible giants who lived on the other side of the island.

Thomas often looked after birds and animals that were sick or injured. Once he brought home a young eagle with a broken wing. He fed and cared for it until the wing had healed. Then he let it go.

Another time, Thomas found an otter with its paw caught in a trap. He set it free.

And whenever Thomas caught fish that were too small, he threw them back into the water.

"Goodbye, fish," he would say. "May you grow big and strong."

Now, Kate, the girl he loved, was the best weaver on the island. She wove beautiful cloth from sheep's wool.

Kate ventured all over the island to collect the moss and lichen she used to dye her wool. But one day, while Thomas was out to sea, the giant found her.

"HA!" he said. "The very person I need to weave me a coat
of nettles. And when you're finished, I shall eat you!"

Thomas had seen everything from his boat and rowed swiftly to shore. He was trying to think of a way to rescue Kate when a great eagle landed before him.

"I saw the giant take the girl," the eagle said. "You helped me once. Now I shall help you."

"Get onto my back and I'll carry you to the giant's castle."
And they flew to the other side of the island.

At last, they could see the castle looming from a cliff overlooking the sea.

"When you get inside, you'll have to search for the girl yourself," the eagle said.

He left Thomas on a window ledge.

Thomas found Kate in the cellar spinning nettles into thread to weave cloth for the giant's coat.

Before they could escape, the giant's wife burst in. "HO!"
she boomed. "Now there are two of you to eat!"

Thomas thought quickly. "Oh, great and beautiful lady,
is there nothing we can give you in return for our freedom?"

The miserly giant never gave his wife gifts. He had never called her beautiful, either.

"I've always wanted a string of pearls," she said. "If you can find me some pearls, I'll free you both." And she let Thomas go.

The boy sat at the edge of the sea. "How am I to find pearls big enough for a giantess?" he wondered aloud.

As he spoke, the sleek head of an otter broke the water in front of him. "I've come to help you as you once helped me," the otter said.

"I'll take you down to the kingdom under the sea. There you'll find the pearls you need." The otter warned the boy not to eat or drink anything while he was in the sea kingdom. "Beware! Not everything is as it seems."

The sea king's daughters came to greet Thomas in front of the palace. They listened to his story, and the eldest princess promised to take him to the cave of pearls.

"But will you not eat something after your long journey?"
she asked. Thomas remembered the otter's warning and
refused.

Then the princess took Thomas's hand and led him to the cave. He quickly gathered up enough pearls to make a necklace for the giant's wife.

"Now that you have the pearls, you must accept a glass of wine," the princess said sweetly. "I made it myself."

Thomas was grateful for her help and felt it would be rude to refuse, so he took a sip. From that moment, he forgot about the real world and everything in it. He had eyes only for the princess.

Meanwhile, Kate, who was allowed out of the castle once a day to pick nettles, was sitting next to a pool talking to the great salmon that lived there.

"The giant's coat is nearly finished," she said, sighing. "Where can Thomas be?"

"You forget nettles sometimes have magic powers," the salmon said. As Kate watched, he took up one that had dropped from her lap, and swam out to sea.

In the sea palace, Thomas was at his wedding banquet, about to marry the princess. But when he saw the salmon carrying the nettle, he remembered Kate and the real world. Suddenly the enchantment of the sea kingdom no longer had power over him.

Thomas saw with horror that the princess was really a sea monster.

"Get onto my back," urged the salmon.

Thomas grabbed the bag of pearls, and the salmon carried him through the sea, up the river, to the pool near the giant's castle.

"I was once a little fish that you threw back," the salmon explained. "I am glad I was able to help you now."

The giant's wife saw Thomas coming and ran out of the castle to meet him. She was so delighted with the pearls that she let Kate go, as she had promised.

Together again, Thomas and Kate lived happily ever after.

But the giant was so angry with his wife that he chased her off the island, and neither of them has been heard of since.

Copyright © 1993 by Fiona Moodie
All rights reserved
Library of Congress catalog card number: 92-56508
Published simultaneously in Canada by HarperCollins*CanadaLtd*
Printed in the United States of America
Designed by Martha Rago
First edition, 1993